Hide and Sheep

Hide and Sheep

by Andrea Beaty

Illustrations by
Bill Mayer

Margaret K. McElderry Books
New York London Toronto Sydney

MARGARET K. McELDERRY BOOKS
An imprint of Simon & Schuster Children's Publishing Division
1230 Avenue of the Americas, New York, New York 10020
Text copyright © 2011 by Andrea Beaty LLC
Illustrations copyright © 2011 by Bill Mayer
MARGARET K. McELDERRY BOOKS is a trademark of Simon & Schuster, Inc.
For information about special discounts for bulk purchases,
please contact Simon & Schuster Special Sales at 1-866-506-1949
or business@simonandschuster.com.
The Simon & Schuster Speakers Bureau can bring authors to your live event.
For more information or to book an event, contact the Simon & Schuster
Speakers Bureau at 1-866-248-3049 or visit our website at
www.simonspeakers.com.
Book design by Lauren Rille and Debra Sfetsios-Conover
The text for this book is set in Alghera.
The illustrations for this book are rendered in pen and watercolor.
Manufactured in China
0311 SCP
10 9 8 7 6 5 4 3 2
Library of Congress Cataloging-in-Publication Data
Beaty, Andrea.
Hide and sheep / Andrea Beaty ; illustrated by Bill Mayer.—1st ed.
p. cm.
Summary: Farmer McFitt must round up his sheep, which have strayed all over
town, in order to shear them to make wool so that he can knit clothing.
ISBN 978-1-4169-2544-6 (hardcover)
[1. Stories in rhyme. 2. Sheep—Fiction. 3. Counting.] I. Mayer, Bill, ill. II. Title.
PZ8.3.B38447Hi 2011
[E]—dc22
2009044809

For Katie, who started it all
—A. B.

For Lee Lee
—B. M.

Wake up! Wake up, Farmer McFitt!
You've sheep to shear and clothes to knit!

Your sheep have grown restless!
They're jumping the gate!
Now wake up and find them before it's too late!

Ten frisky lambs run away to the zoo
to meet an okapi, a kind kangaroo,
a spotted giraffe with his head in the trees.
They hang out and play with the wild chimpanzees.

Nine join the circus
and dance with a bear,
get shot from a cannon,
and fly through the air.
Like woolly white comets
they soar ever higher.
They take one last bow
from atop the high wire.

"Play ball!" cries the umpire as eight sheep trot in.
They nibble the outfield and sheepishly grin.

They know it's forbidden but munch all the same.
With three chomps they're out of the old baseball game!

Seven sly lambkins are eager to go.
They sneak to the village to take in a show.

Alone in the dark with their favorite flick,
they gobble down popcorn until they feel sick.

Six clever sheep
in the new art museum.
Some pose like a statue
so no one will see 'em.

Hooves click on marble.
They dance and they play
with Salvador Dalí, van Gogh,
and Monet.

Five groovy lambs hit the beach for the day.
With surfboard and snorkles, they're ready to play.
They do the Beach Boogie and try to get tanned
like all of the tourists asleep on the sand.

Four hungry ewes run off looking for snacks.
They roam the library, inspecting the stacks.

Novels and poetry! All of it free!
They nosh and they nibble from A down to Z.

Three naughty sheep on a tour of the town
stop by to visit with Fireman Brown.
When the tour's over, those wicked lambs hide.
They crank up the siren and go for a ride!

Two silly brothers with nothing to do
find an old bicycle built just for two.
They zoom down the sidewalk, so fast and so free,
don't look where they're going and land in a tree!

One little lamb with its snow-colored wool
follows young Mary and heads into school.
The farmer comes creeping. It's too late to run!
CLIP! CLIP! And SNIP! Now the shearing is done!

Hip! Hip! Hurray!
For Farmer McFitt!
Your sheep are sheared!
Their clothes are knit!

You've dressed your flock from toe to head.
Now stop counting sheep . . .

it's time for bed.